COLLECTION MANAGEMENT

6/25/14	3 - 2	2/3/14

DAMIAN DROOTH SUPERSLEUTH

THE MYSTERY OF THE MISSING MUTTS

by Barbara Mitchelhill

illustrated by Tony Ross

STONE ARCH BOOKS
www.stonearchbooks.com

First published in the United States in 2009
by Stone Arch Books
151 Good Counsel Drive, P.O. Box 669
Mankato, Minnesota 56002
www.stonearchbooks.com

First published in 2008
by Andersen Press Ltd, London

Library of Congress Cataloging-in-Publication Data
Mitchelhill, Barbara.
    [Dog snatchers]
    The Mystery of the Missing Mutts / by Barbara Mitchelhill; illustrated
by Tony Ross.
        p. cm. — (Pathway Books) (Damian Drooth Supersleuth)
        Originally published: Dog snatchers. London: Andersen, 2008.
        ISBN 978-1-4342-1216-0 (library binding)
        [1. Mystery and detective stories. 2. Dogs—Fiction.] I. Ross, Tony, ill.
II. Title.
PZ7.M697My 2009
[Fic]—dc22   2008031825

Summary: Dog snatchers have been nabbing mutts all over town, but
Damian Drooth is on the case! With the help of his group of trainee
detectives, Damian is determined to find out what's happened to the missing
pups. For some detectives, this case could be uncrackable — but not for
Damian Drooth!

Creative Director: Heather Kindseth
Graphic Designer: Emily Harris

J'Fic

1 2 3 4 5 6 14 13 12 11 10 09

Printed in the United States of America

Table of Contents

Chapter 1

You probably already know who I am. Damian Drooth, Supersleuth and Ace Detective. I'm famous around here. People come from miles around to ask for my help.

I'm going to tell you about a crime I solved just last week. It wasn't easy. It took all my brainpower and smarts to crack this case.

It all started Saturday morning.

All of my friends were in my garden shed for our detective classes. I was explaining how to spot criminal disguises, like wigs and dark glasses.

"My grandpa has a wig," said Lavender. "He doesn't have any hair."

"Your grandpa could be lying," I said. "He probably has tons of hair. I bet he's really a criminal. He doesn't want to be spotted by the police. That's why he wears a wig."

Lavender started crying. I wasn't surprised. It's hard to learn the truth, especially when you're only six.

I kept talking over her noisy crying. But just then, someone knocked on the shed door. Everyone — even Lavender — got quiet. I went to see who it was.

I opened the door. An old lady was standing there. She was small and had white curly hair.

"Hello," she said. "Are you Damian Drooth?"

"Who's asking?" I said. I didn't want to give anything away.

"I'm Mrs. Popperwell," the old lady said.

I was suspicious. I'd never heard that name before. It was probably fake — her hair looked like a wig to me. I would have to be careful.

"Why are you looking for Damian Drooth?" I asked.

She took a tissue from her handbag. "Because Blossom is missing," she said. She wiped away tears (which might have been fake).

"Missing?" I asked.

"For two hours already," Mrs. Popperwell told me.

"That's not so long," I said.

"My Blossom never goes out," she said, sobbing. "Not without me."

"That's kind of weird," I said. "Most girls like to go out and play with their friends."

"She's not a girl," Mrs. Popperwell said. "She's a dog, and I'm just so worried about her."

"So why didn't you go to the police?" I asked.

"Because I've heard that Damian Drooth is a brilliant detective," Mrs. Popperwell said. "People say he's better than the police. Much better! They say he can solve any crime."

She was clearly somebody who appreciated me. I took off my baseball cap and my shades to reveal my face.

"I am Damian Drooth," I said.

Her eyes opened wide in surprise. I could tell she was really impressed.

"Sorry about all the questions, Mrs. Popperwell, but you can't be too careful in the detective business," I explained.

I invited her to come inside. Then I found a box for her to sit on.

"You'd better tell me all about Blossom and when she went missing," I said.

It turned out that Mrs. Popperwell had let her dog out in her yard that morning.

"When I called Blossom to come back in, she wasn't there. She had disappeared," Mrs. Popperwell said. She blew her nose. I think she was pretty upset.

I ate some chips while I thought about the problem.

"Well, it sounds to me like there are Dognappers in the area," I said finally, looking at Mrs. Popperwell.

Mrs. Popperwell turned as white as a sheet. "Dognappers?" she gasped. "What are they?"

"They are people who kidnap dogs," I explained. "You'll probably get a letter soon demanding a lot of money."

I thought Mrs. Popperwell was going
to faint. I offered her a chip to calm her
down. "Don't worry, Mrs. Popperwell,"
I said. "I'll put my detectives on the
case. They'll track down the criminals
in no time."

Chapter 2

My friend Winston lived on Richmond Road, just around the corner from Mrs. Popperwell and her dog.

"I've seen Blossom a few times," Winston told me. "She's a poodle with white curly hair. She looks a lot like Mrs. Popperwell."

"That information could be useful," I said, writing it in my detective's notebook. "But I have a plan."

"Already?" said Todd.

"You're brilliant, Damian," said Lavender. She had stopped crying by then. "You're going to save Mrs. Popperwell's doggie because you have the best brain in the whole world."

I liked Lavender. Nice kid.

"Here's my plan," I said to my friends. "We make posters and stick them on telephone poles and store windows around town. A hundred should be enough."

Everybody thought it was a good plan.

"How do we get 100 posters, Damian?" Winston asked.

"We'll make one," I said. "Then we'll copy it on my mom's copy machine. It won't take long."

In fact, it took us forever to make the poster. We put Mrs. Popperwell's phone number at the bottom. That was so we could go to her house and wait for witnesses to call.

This was the poster:

This dog has been stolen
by dangerous Dognappers.

Have you seen anything suspicious?
Call 555-0812
BIG REWARD!

Once the poster was finished, I ran into the house. Mom was upstairs cleaning the bathroom.

I didn't want to bother her, so I didn't ask if I could use the copy machine.

I knew she wouldn't mind. It was for a good cause.

I went into the dining room, turned the machine on, and slipped the poster under the lid.

It's a really old machine. If you're not careful, it flings the copies out and you have to catch them. It's also really noisy.

That day, Mom must have heard the whirring noise. "Damian!" she said as she came bursting into the dining room. "I've told you before not to use that copy machine!"

I jumped. When I turned around, the copies starting flying off the machine like leaves off a tree.

"It's for a good cause," I explained. "A little poodle is missing. I'm saving it from Dognappers."

Any nice person would have understood. They would have felt sorry for the poor animal. But Mom was not in a good mood.

"The police deal with lost dogs," she said. "Turn that copy machine off now."

I tried to explain about how upset Mrs. Popperwell was, but Mom wouldn't listen. She was really crabby. She marched over to the copy machine and unplugged it.

"I've told you not to use it, Damian," she said. "Don't waste my paper for one of your detective games! Now go out and play with your friends."

Did I hear right? Did she think this was all a game? Did she think we were just playing like little kids? I tried to pick up the posters, but she went crazy.

"Go!" she shouted. "Now!"

I had to leave without my posters.

But I didn't give up on my plan.

Chapter 3

"So you didn't get a single poster?" Winston asked.

I shook my head. "It was a difficult situation," I said. "Mom was in one of her moods. I had to get out fast."

"So what do we do now?" Harry asked.

"We'll just have to make the posters ourselves," I said.

They all groaned.

I could tell they weren't used to hard work.

"That's only twenty-five each," I said. "It won't take you long."

Todd, who is really good at math, told me I was wrong. "There are five of us," he said. "That means twenty each."

He didn't understand how to run a detective agency. "Somebody has to be in charge," I explained. "And I'm the only trained detective."

I won't bother to tell you what happened next. Once the argument was over, I agreed to help them make posters. Just for the sake of solving the crime.

"We'll need five pencils," said Harry, "and a hundred sheets of paper."

"We all have pencils," said Lavender. "We could use our detective notebooks."

"Your detective notebooks won't work," I said. "We need big sheets of plain paper for posters." That was a problem. Mom had already kicked me out of the house, so I couldn't get any paper.

"I have an idea," Harry said. "My dad got a bunch of posters yesterday. He was complaining about them. I'm pretty sure they're not important. He'll be glad to get rid of them."

"What's your point, Harry?" I asked.

"Well, they're only printed on one side. We could use the back!" Harry said.

That was just what we needed. I sent Harry to get them. Ten minutes later, he was back, carrying a huge box stuffed full of posters.

The posters were very boring. I could see why his dad didn't want them. They had a photo of a strange woman with frizzy hair, and then underneath it said, "Vote for Peacock." Who would be interested in that? Nobody, that's who.

Finding Blossom was a lot more important. We turned the posters over and started writing on the blank side.

We wrote: "This dog has been stolen by dangerous Dognappers." Then we did a drawing of Blossom, like before. But writing a lot of posters was hard. Our hands began to hurt. It was really hard to do our best writing.

"My fingers hurt," said Winston.

"Mine too," said Todd.

"Mine three," said Lavender.

In the end, we kept it simple. We did four posters each, except for Lavender, who did seven.

Then we headed to town. We threw the extra posters in a dumpster. A few blew away, but it couldn't be helped.

We stuck our missing dog posters on every telephone pole down Main Street and on the grocery store's window. I had a tube of superglue, so they all stuck really well.

The man from the grocery store didn't seem to like it. He ran out of the store, shouting, "What do you think you're doing?"

We didn't hang around. I knew he'd understand when he read the poster. He might even be able to give us some information.

After that, we went straight to Mrs. Popperwell's house to tell her how we were dealing with her case. She was very interested to hear what we had done.

"Posters! That's a great idea," she said. "How kind of you."

We sat by the phone and waited for people to call with information about Blossom and her kidnappers. Mrs. Popperwell brought us cookies and cake to help us keep our strength up.

But after one package of cookies, several jelly doughnuts, and one chocolate cake, there hadn't been a single call.

This was bad. Very bad. How could we solve the crime without some help from the public? Action was needed.

Chapter 4

Then I had a great idea. "We'll use a decoy," I said.

"What's that?" Harry asked.

So I explained, "We'll let another dog loose near Mrs. Popperwell's house."

"Why?" Winston asked.

"Because that's where the Dognappers are working," I said. "We'll wait for them to take the decoy dog."

"Then we call the police," said Lavender.

"Yes," I said. Lavender understood. She was smart. She'll make a great detective one day.

"But how do we get a decoy dog?" Harry asked.

"You can use Thumper," said Winston. "He'll walk up and down the street just as long as there are no cats to chase."

"We can't use Thumper," I said.

"Why not?" Winston asked.

"Think about it, Winston," I said. "Thumper is dirty and scruffy and he smells. Who would want to steal him?"

Winston got quiet, but I think he understood.

Instead, we used Todd and Lavender's dog, Curly. She wouldn't win a Top Dog Contest, but she was the best we had.

Todd went to get Curly. Mrs. Popperwell made us a few sandwiches.

By the time Todd came back with his dog on its leash, we had finished them. Delicious!

We got up to leave.

"Thanks, Mrs. Popperwell," I said. "Let us know if you get any phone calls or any letters asking for money."

"I will," said Mrs. Popperwell as she waved us off down the street.

"What's the plan, Damian?" Winston asked when we got outside.

"First, we'll release Curly," I said. "Then we'll spread out along the street. Keep your eyes on her, but try to stay hidden."

"How do we do that?" Harry asked.

"There are plenty of bushes around here," I told him. "Use your detective skills. Crouch down behind the bushes so the Dognappers won't see you."

This was really exciting. Todd unclipped the leash. Curly trotted off. She took off down the street.

We hid and watched from behind the bushes. Curly was a great decoy dog.

Just when things were going great, people saw us in their yards. They got mad. We didn't want to leave our good hiding spots.

Then they started to get upset. They threw us out.

I tried explaining that we were working undercover, but it was no good. We had to stand on the sidewalk, where anyone could see us (including the Dognappers).

It's a tough life being a detective.

Just as I was wondering where we could hide, things suddenly began to happen.

A man wearing a cap and a large overcoat (could this be a disguise?) came down the street.

He called to Curly. "Here, dog! Good girl! Come see what I have," he said. He had a dog biscuit in his hand to tempt her.

I alerted my friends right away.

Curly is a very friendly dog. She went right up to the man.

He pulled the belt off his coat. Then he attached it to Curly's collar.

"That's him!" I said. "He's a Dognapper."

Lavender burst into tears. She yelled, "That man has my doggie!"

I had to get Todd to keep Lavender quiet. I didn't want the Dognapper to know he was about to be caught.

"What do we do now, Damian?" asked Harry.

"You go back to Mrs. Popperwell's," I said. "Call the police. We'll follow the Dognapper."

"But how can I tell them where to look for him?" Harry asked. "You don't know where he'll go."

Harry was right. "Forget it," I said. "We'll all follow him and see what happens. We don't need help from the police, do we?"

Chapter 5

We were on the trail of the Dognapper. He started heading for Main Street.

"Smart," I said. "Very smart."

"What is?" Winston asked.

"He probably parked his car in the parking ramp," I told him. "We'll have to stop him before he drives off with Curly. She could be lost forever."

Lavender started crying again.

"I'll never see my doggie again!"
she said.

Todd found a piece of candy in
his pocket. That shut Lavender up for
a while.

"We'll have to catch up with him," I
said. "Even if he realizes we're on
his trail."

We all raced down Main Street
toward the Dognapper. By the time he
reached the grocery store, we were close
behind him.

Luckily, he stopped to talk to the owner,
who had been trying to scrape our posters
off the window.

That gave me my chance.

"Call the police," I yelled to the owner.

I grabbed the belt out of the Dognapper's hand. "This man stole our dog," I yelled. "And it's definitely not the first time he's done this kind of thing. Call 911."

I could tell that the Dognapper was shocked at being caught by a bunch of kids. He just stood there, his mouth wide open, while Lavender pounded him with her little fists. She yelled, "You mean man! You stole my doggie."

When Curly realized that she was safe, she started barking and jumping up on Todd. She was really glad to see him. A group of people stopped to see what was going on. There was a big crowd.

But the owner of the grocery store wasn't very helpful. He didn't call 911. In fact, he was pretty rude.

"Wasn't it you kids who stuck these posters on my windows?" he said.

I was shocked! No wonder nobody had called Mrs. Popperwell with information. The owner of the grocery store had removed most of our posters.

The next thing that happened was really lucky. A policeman spotted the crowd and came running. He probably thought there was a bank robbery or something.

I explained as quickly as I could. "My name is Damian Drooth, and these are my trainee detectives," I said.

"Damian's famous," Winston added. "He works for Inspector Crockitt."

The policeman looked down at us, tapping his chin with his finger.

"Damian Drooth, huh?" he said. "Well, I'm Officer Nobbs. I don't believe Inspector Crockitt has ever mentioned you."

I must admit I was very surprised to hear that. "Take my word for it," I said. "And believe me when I say that this man is a Dognapper. You should question him about a dog named Blossom who belongs to Mrs. Popperwell. She's missing."

Officer Nobbs didn't pay attention. He just looked at Curly. "So who does this dog belong to?" he asked.

"It's my doggie," said Lavender.

"And mine," said Todd. "This girl's my sister."

The Dognapper looked very nervous. That was a sure sign of a guilty person.

"I'm sorry, Officer," he said. "I'm on business in the area and I saw this dog wandering up and down the road. It was obviously lost. I was worried that it might get run over. I thought I should take it to the police station."

A likely story! But the policeman believed him.

"That's all right," Officer Nobbs said. Then he turned to us and said, "Run along, kids, and remember to keep your dog in your yard next time."

I couldn't believe it! We had caught the Dognapper right in the act of dognapping. We had handed him over to the police. And then the police had let him go. Is that scary or what? No dog was safe. A terrible criminal was on the loose again.

So what should we do?

Chapter 6

"Every dog in this town is in danger," I explained to my friends as we walked away. "We must protect them until the Dognapper is behind bars."

"He's a mean man," Lavender said, sobbing.

I patted her on the head. "Yes, he's a mean man all right," I said. "But don't worry, Lavender. I'll have him arrested by dinner."

My plan was to look out for any dogs in danger.

I would make sure they were off the streets for a few hours, until I had more proof of the Dognapper's criminal activities. All of my friends would go down different streets looking for wandering dogs.

"Can I come with you, Damian?" Lavender asked. She didn't want to go on her own. I didn't mind. She could watch me, and she'd learn more that way.

"What'll we do with all the dogs?" Harry asked.

"We'll take them back to my house," I said. "They can go in the shed. They'll be safe there."

We took off, looking for dogs.

Luckily, I had my
binoculars in my
pocket. I wouldn't
miss a thing.

I found the first
dog in a convertible
on Long Street. It
had been left there all alone. I looked
around for the owner, but I couldn't
see anyone.

"I'll leave a note," I said to Lavender.
I pulled out my detective's notebook
and wrote:

Your dog
has been
moved to

34 Harris Street.

Damian Drooth,

Detective

We scooped the dog up and carried it away. Luckily it was only a little black Scottie dog. It wasn't too heavy.

Before we reached my street, I saw another one. This dog was tied up near the corner store. If the Dognapper came along, it would be easy to take him.

"Maybe the owner is in the store," said Lavender.

"Maybe, but maybe not," I said.

"Go see, Damian," Lavender said.

Just to make her happy, I poked my head inside. There were three people — a man behind the counter and a man and a woman buying some dog food.

"Excuse me," I said. "I'm Damian Drooth, detective. Do you realize that the town is on high alert today?"

They turned around and looked at me as if I was something from outer space. I had probably shocked them. Maybe it was the sight of a black Scottie tucked under my arm.

Maybe they had never seen a detective before.

I tried again, speaking more slowly. "There is a Dognapper on the prowl. I wondered if you knew about it," I said.

They laughed. Then they shook their heads. "No," said the woman. "We haven't seen a Dognapper. Not around here, anyway."

They turned back and kept putting cans into a grocery bag. It was obvious to my trained eye that the dog outside wasn't theirs.

"Let's go, Lavender," I said when I came out of the store. "They don't know anything."

Lavender untied the leash from the drainpipe.

I wrote another note and stuck it on the wall. Then we took off.

By the time we reached my back yard, there was a lot of barking coming from the shed. That was good news. My friends must have found dogs out on the streets.

The dogs were safe for now. I needed to convince the police that the Dognapper was roaming our town. How was I going to do that?

Chapter 7

"We're back," I shouted as I opened the shed door. The shed was crammed full of dogs. Just then, a German shepherd dog jumped out.

"He's huge," I said. "He's the size of a donkey."

"I know," said Harry. "I found him out in a yard on Tree Street. He didn't want to come at first, but I had a sandwich in my pocket."

"Good work, Harry," I said. "The owners will be grateful when they learn how you saved him."

Winston had found two dogs in the park. Todd had rescued a spaniel from outside the Community Center.

"They did great," said Lavender.

"They did," I said. "At any minute the Dognapper could have come along and taken these dogs."

We sat down and had some chips.

Winston decided he had to go home and get Thumper. "I'm worried about him," Winston said. "I left him in our back yard. You never know — he could get snatched."

Winston left and we finished our chips.

"What do we do next?" Todd asked. "We can't keep the dogs here forever."

"First things first," I said. "They need food and water. I'll go get some."

The German shepherd had been having a great time in the garden. As I left the shed, he came running over to meet me.

Although he was big, he was very friendly. He jumped up and down and then ran in circles.

He flattened Mom's plants, but I didn't think she'd mind. She likes dogs.

He followed me to the back door. "Stay!" I said and he sat down all right but he started barking. Big dogs have really loud barks. I just hoped Mom wouldn't hear him.

In the kitchen, I found some bowls and filled a bottle with water. There were two cans of meat in the pantry. They would be perfect for the dogs' dinners. I was just looking in a drawer for the can opener when the phone rang. I ignored it. Mom would pick it up in the bedroom.

It was not easy, carrying all the doggie things. As I opened the door, the German shepherd burst in, still barking. He bumped right into me and the cans flew out of my hands.

So did the dishes, and they smashed on the floor. I tried to calm down the dog, but he wouldn't stop barking.

Then Mom walked in. "What on earth is that dog doing in here?" she shouted.

The German shepherd seemed pleased to see her, too. He jumped up. That made Mom stagger back until she was pinned against the door.

"Get him off me!" she yelled.

I did my best, but it wasn't easy. It took a while for me to push him out into the yard.

Mom was not in a good mood. I have noticed lately that she gets easily upset. Maybe she needs a vacation. Disney World would be good.

"Damian, listen to me!" she shouted. "Why is this animal in my yard? And why do I keep getting phone calls from people accusing me of taking their dogs?

"What's going on, Damian?"

Luckily, just then there was a knock at the front door. Mom went to see who it was. It turned out to be Officer Nobbs, who we'd met outside the grocery store. Mom brought him into the kitchen.

Apparently, a man in the park had seen Winston walk off with his dog and had called the police. I thought that was pretty sneaky.

"I guessed it might have something to do with you, Damian," said Officer Nobbs. "I thought the boy in the park might be one of your friends. Dognapping is a crime."

I protested, "Winston wasn't dognapping. He is one of my trainee detectives. We are saving all the local dogs who are in danger from the Dognapper."

Mom turned pale.

"So where is the dog now?" Officer Nobbs asked.

"In the shed," I explained.

"And Winston?" Officer Nobbs asked.

"He went out to save another dog," I told him.

The policeman walked outside and headed toward the shed. I guess he was really excited to see the dogs. But before he got there, Winston walked into the yard.

Bad timing! Was he about to be arrested?

Chapter 8

I couldn't believe what I saw. Winston was standing there holding two leashes. One belonged to Thumper. The other belonged to a white poodle.

"You found Blossom!" I yelled. "Great detective work, Winston. I'll call Mrs. Popperwell."

I didn't wait. I ran back to the house and called her right away. She was thrilled to know her dog was safe.

"You are wonderful, Damian," she said. "Who else could have found her so quickly? You saved my baby from the Dognapper. I will come over right away to get her."

I would have told Mom the good news, but she was in the living room talking to a visitor. Just as I was about to go out the back door, she called out, "Damian! Do you know anything about some posters?"

I didn't say anything. "Come here, please," she yelled. "Now!"

I didn't have time to stop. I had to go back outside.

Officer Nobbs had finished asking Winston questions. He was about to go into the shed. He should have waited before opening the door. But he didn't.

Thumper and Blossom ran to join the other dogs in the shed. The German shepherd followed them. They all pushed Officer Nobbs into the shed.

Our shed is not very big. Several dogs, five kids, and a policeman is too many things in the shed. The dogs were barking and jumping and having a great time. Officer Nobbs should have stayed calm, that's what I say. I don't think he knew how to handle dogs. He panicked. That's why he ended up on the floor.

Then Mom arrived with her visitor, a weird lady named Mrs. Peacock. She wasn't at all interested in our detective work. She kept talking about how her posters were blowing all around the town and were ruined. What posters?

But then Mrs. Popperwell arrived. Good old Mrs. Popperwell. She wouldn't listen to a word Mrs. Peacock or Officer Nobbs said.

"This boy is a genius," Mrs. Popperwell said. "You must be so proud of him, Mrs. Drooth."

Mom seemed really mad at me. Mrs. Popperwell didn't notice.

"Thank you so much, Damian," she continued. "How did you find my dear little Blossom?"

I didn't have time to tell her that Winston had found her. I thought I'd tell her another day.

"I'd like to have you all over for a party tomorrow," Mrs. Popperwell told us.

"There will be some important people coming to meet you," she said to me. "I want everyone to know how smart you are."

Mrs. Popperwell left with Blossom. Mrs. Peacock left with a few posters that had been lying in the corner of the shed. Officer Nobbs left looking very dirty. I don't think Inspector Crockitt would be happy to see one of his officers with his uniform all torn up like that.

Then a bunch of people came to collect the other dogs.

I told them that they shouldn't let their dogs loose in the town. All dogs deserve to be safe from Dognappers, that's what I think.

Chapter 9

Mrs. Popperwell's party was great. There was tons of food. I especially liked the giant sausage rolls and the chocolate cake.

When we were finished eating, Mrs. Popperwell gave a speech. "Ladies and gentlemen," she said, "I would like you to meet the finest detective in town — Damian Drooth. He and his trainee detectives saved my Blossom from the evil Dognapper."

Everybody cheered (except Mom, who was still mad at me for all the mess in the yard).

Inspector Crockitt was at the party too. It turned out that he was Mrs. Popperwell's nephew. After her speech, he came over to me.

"My aunt seems very pleased with you, Damian," Inspector Crockitt said. "But one of my officers tells me that you've been stealing dogs. I don't like the sound of that."

I smiled and helped myself to another sausage roll. "I was working undercover," I explained.

"Undercover?" Inspector Crockitt replied. "As what?"

I tapped my nose and winked.

"Top secret," I said. "But we got rid of the Dognapper, I think."

"Who?" Inspector Crockitt asked.

I was surprised his officer hadn't passed on the information. "Don't worry," I said. "He won't dare to come back. Now he knows we have a team of young detectives on the job."

"What job?" Inspector Crockitt asked.

"Dog protection," I told him.

Inspector Crockitt frowned. "You and your detective work," he growled. "This time, I'll pretend this didn't happen. But watch it, or you'll be in big trouble!" Then he walked away.

When I finally got the chance to talk to Winston, I asked him where he had found Blossom.

I was surprised by what he told me.

"She was in my back yard with Thumper," he said. "She must have jumped the fence. They really like each other, you know."

"You mean she got away from the Dognapper?" I asked.

Winston shook his head and said, "No, Damian. Don't you get it? Blossom wasn't dognapped. She was in our back yard the whole time. There never was a Dognapper."

I wasn't convinced.

I looked around to see if anyone was listening. Then I whispered, "Don't say a word, Winston. Nobody needs to know how you found her. Keep it to yourself, okay? It's for the best."

Several weeks later, Blossom surprised everybody by having five puppies. They looked like little Thumpers.

I asked Mom if I could have one of the puppies as a guard dog, but she said no. She said she had enough work keeping me under control. I don't understand that. But I will keep on trying.

About the Author

Barbara Mitchelhill started writing when she was seven years old. She says, "When I was eight or nine, I used to pretend I was a detective, just like Damian. My friend Liz and I used to watch people walking down our street and we would write clues in our notebooks. I don't remember catching any criminals!" She has written many books for children. She lives in Staffordshire, England, and writes her books in her wonderful study overlooking fields of sheep. She has a dog named Ella.

About the Illustrator

Tony Ross was born in London in 1938. He has illustrated lots of books, including some by Paula Danziger, Michael Palin, and Roald Dahl. He also writes and illustrates his own books. He has worked as a cartoonist, graphic designer, and art director of an advertising agency. When he was a kid, he wanted to grow up to be a cowboy.

Glossary

appreciated (uh-PREE-shee-ate-id)—understood and admired

brilliant (BRIL-yuhnt)—very smart

criminal (KRIM-uh-nuhl)—someone who commits a crime

decoy (DEE-koy)—something that lures a person into a trap

disguises (diss-GIZES)—if people are wearing disguises, they are dressed in a way that hides who they are

genius (JEEN-yuss)—if you are a genius, you are very smart

information (in-fur-MAY-shuhn)—facts and knowledge

reveal (ri-VEEL)—to make known

suspicious (suh-SPISH-uhss)—if you feel suspicious, you think something is wrong

trainee (tray-NEE)—someone who is learning something

undercover (uhn-dur-CUV-ur)—doing secret work

witness (WIT-niss)—a person who has seen or heard something

Discussion Questions

1. Damian says there are Dognappers, but Winston says there aren't. What do you think really happened?

2. At the end of this book, Damian asks his mom if he can have a puppy. If you have a pet, what are some things that you need to do to take care of your pet?

3. Damian is teaching the other kids how to be detectives. Do you think he's doing a good job? Why or why not?

Writing Prompts

1. Do you have a pet? Write about your pet. If you don't have one, write about a pet you would like to have.

2. Damian and his friends solve mysteries. What do you do with your friends? Write about something that you and your friends like to do.

3. This book is a mystery story. Write your own mystery story!

Internet Sites

Do you want to know more about subjects related to this book? Or are you interested in learning about other topics? Then check out FactHound, a fun, easy way to find Internet sites.

Our investigative staff has already sniffed out great sites for you!

Here's how to use FactHound:

1. Visit *www.facthound.com*

2. Select your grade level.

3. To learn more about subjects related to this book, type in the book's ISBN number: **9781434212160**

4. Click the **Fetch It** button.

FactHound will fetch the best Internet sites for you!